Soror Love

Shaun J. Phree

Published by PLE Press LLC, 2024.

Also by Shaun J. Phree

Chocolate Caramel Vanilla
Caramel Addiction
Vanilla Fetish
Chocolate Obsession

Standalone
No Love Lost: A Poetic Tale
10 Steps to Self Care
Her Mother, My Love
Never
Soror Love
Writer's Surge
Classified

Table of Contents

Chapter 1

People flooded the hotel lobby, dragging their suitcases and trying to find their way to their rooms. Lauren pulled her black suitcase behind her, adjusting her white and pale pink cocktail dress on her beautifully sculpted body, while she slid between guests towards the front desk. She'd attended many national conventions over the years, but this one differed slightly. Nu Nu Lambda Sorority was Lauren's baby, and just like a single dad in a grocery store with an adorable toddler, this baby attracted the attention of beautiful women. She vowed to keep the national convention clear of her flings, and for a decade, she'd succeeded.

She slapped her wallet on the hotel front desk, catching the attention of the front desk agent, a blonde, heavily tanned, early 20-something tall, thin stud with a short haircut.

"Welcome to the Renaissance Carlton Hotel. I'm Jyn. How can I help you?" she asked.

"I'm Lauren Jacobson," she pushed her license and a printout of her reservation across the desk towards Jyn. She quickly turned around and scanned the lobby, taking count of her sorority sisters. *Why is there always a lesbian at the hotel's front desk when we have events?* Her sorority was mislabeled as a lesbian sorority when most of her members identified as everything but lesbian.

"Yes, Ms. Jacobson. We have your king suite ready with the additional requests fulfilled," Jyn returned Lauren's license and added two room keys to the desk. She caught Lauren's eyes and locked on, "Is there anything else I...I can do for you?"

"Hmph, well, thank you...Jyn is it," Lauren glanced at the small name tag attached to the white button-down, hugging Jyn's chest.

"It is. And it has been my pleasure to help you. If you need anything, anything at all, let me know," Jyn held Lauren's hand and lingered for a moment. Lauren laughed Jyn's hand off, snatched her room keys and license from the desk, and smiled before walking away. She stopped in the middle of the lobby and took a deep breath. These were her people. Her organization. All here for something she created.

"Ladies!" she announced across the lobby, catching the attention of women of diverse ages and races, all wearing a similar shade of soft pink. "Welcome to the 2024 Nu Nu Lambda Sorority, Innnnnnnnnnnncorporated Biennial National Convention!"

The lobby roared with stilettos stomping on the marble floor and clapping in unison. Yet it all instantly silenced with Lauren's hand in the air above them all.

"If this is your first National Convention or if you are intake, please visit the registration table to the left." Lauren pointed to the large table covered with a soft pink tablecloth. Folders, checklists, and sisters' gifts were neatly arranged in front of three smiling women.

"For my prophytes," the hotel lobby roared with the sorority call, "well, you know what to do!" Lauren waved her hand to the small round check-in table to her right, covered in a white satin tablecloth with only sisters' gifts decorating it; one woman sitting behind the table didn't bother to look up at Lauren; she continued to swipe through her phone. Lauren was annoyed by the lack of enthusiasm and quickly wrapped things up, "I will see you tonight, in the streets of Miami, for the Intake' Night of Flames."

Lauren didn't wait for the applause to stop; she moved swiftly through the ladies towards the prophyte table. Before she could reach the uninterested young woman, a tall, brown-skinned plus sized woman with a long black weave dancing on her lower back grabbed the young woman by her arm, forced her to stand up, and pushed her away from the table before sitting in the chair with a large smile on her face staring directly at Lauren coming towards her.

"Hey there, President Jacobson, how are you?" she smiled slyly, pushing a sister's gift into Lauren's hands "Are you here for your sister's gift?"

"Kelsey, you know why I'm here; otherwise, you wouldn't be here," Lauren scolded. "Thank you for my gift, but you know I don't take one," she waved off the heavily detailed gift bag and turned her back to the table. With her arms crossed, she took in her flock.

"Your ass looks particularly delicious in that dress," Kelsey whispered just behind Lauren's ear while leaning on the small table.

The hairs on Lauren's neck stood at attention as Kelsey's breath tickled them. She fought off a smile, shook off the heat, and made sure no one was paying attention to them.

"Down, girl," Lauren responded. A familiar form caught her eye across the lobby. Before walking away, she grabbed her bag, glanced back at Kelsey, and whispered, "My room, midnight."

Kelsey sat down as she watched her president disappear in the crowd. She couldn't wait to put her face between her president's legs, but now she had to worry about the flood of prophytes headed her way.

Lauren greeted her sorors by shaking hands, patting shoulders, and tossing smiles. Then there was Janelle. Janelle stood directly in Lauren's path, adjusting her dress, perfecting her pose, and waiting for Lauren's eyes. Instead, Lauren directed her attention to another soror.

"Hey, sis," Lauren turned to her left and hugged a thin, caramel complexion woman with brown dreadlocks settled on her shoulders. "How are you, Tiffany?"

"I'm well and getting better by the day," Tiffany said with a calming glance toward the wide-eyed Janelle frozen in the lobby. "How are you, President?"

Janelle adjusted her fitted, soft pink, and black mini dress, slid off the six-inch pink stiletto heels, and headed towards the hotel's restaurant bar. *This was pointless.* Lauren glanced at Janelle's full, supple bottom glide into the restaurant. *She'd pay for that.*

"I am stressed as always," Lauren returned her attention to Tiffany. "Will my Executive Director have some time to run through this weekend, tonight? All I need is ten minutes."

"That's no problem. I will be at your door at 8 pm. I have a date at 8:30, so that's perfect." Tiffany knew Lauren's reputation and admired her as a sorority leader but stayed clear of being alone with her. Too many sorors started their sorority career, turning their nose up at Lauren, but ended up in her bed. She didn't understand why so many of them flocked to Lauren. Most thought Lauren's caramel complexion face was plain. Tiffany would have blamed the attention on Lauren's body because she'd recently lost 100 pounds, but these women fell for her way before that.

"Hmph, a date, huh? It must be one of the bruhs if it's this evening," Lauren pried. She never pinpointed Tiffany's preferences since she didn't bring dates to events or post anyone on social media.

"Miami is a big city with a lot of highways coming in and out and even an airport for people to fly in," Tiffany laughed Lauren off sarcastically. "I will see you later, President."

"Bye, Tiffany," Lauren responded as she walked away. *I need to find Janelle before she has too many drinks. Things never turned out well when these women poured liquor on their broken hearts.* She headed towards the restaurant; as she walked past the front doors, stomping and chanting grew louder. It was the bruhs. She decided to hang out and wait for their entrance.

Six masculine women dressed in assorted t-shirts, navy blue timberland boots, black jeans, jackets with fraternity letters, line names, and crossing years extravagantly embroidered on their backs and sleeves stomped into the hotel, flashing their fraternity hand sign.

"Welcome, bruhs, from the sorors of Nu Nu Lambda Sorority, Innnnnnnnncorporated!" Lauren yelled as the crowd turned their attention toward her. "We can't wait to see what you all have in store for us this weekend!"

The bruhs of Nu Delta Xi Fraternity were quickly quieted by a light-skinned masculine woman with a short haircut, "We'd like to thank you, President Jacobson, and all the ladies of Nu Nu Lambda Sorority!"

All the women in the lobby cheered and celebrated as they gathered around the bruhs. Lauren quickly slipped into the restaurant before she could be distracted again. She found Janelle sitting barefoot at the bar, laughing with a bruh. Janelle sat before an empty shot glass and a half-empty tequila sunrise.

"Hey Janelle, and PHenox, right," Lauren pointed towards the smiling, light-skinned lesbian stud wearing jet-black locs with her hand creeping up Janelle's bare thigh.

"Yes, President Jacobson, nice to see you again. You can call me Brittani," the stud responded without a glance from Lauren. Janelle smiled at her as Lauren burned a hole in the back of her head.

"Same, but you can keep calling me President Jacobson. Would you mind leaving me and Janelle for a moment? We need to run over some sorority business," Lauren lied. The stud's eyes darted between Janelle and Lauren. It didn't seem like either lady was paying her any attention at that moment.

Janelle turned around to face Lauren. She adjusted her breasts in her fitted dress as she stared into Lauren's eyes, "Hi there, President Jacobson; nice to see you again."

"What are you doing?" Lauren asked quietly as she pulled up a bar stool, so close the tiny hairs on their arms touched.

"I'm having a drink with one of my bruhs. What are you doing?" Janelle responded with a giggle. She was tired of being Lauren's play toy whenever she wanted to pull her out.

"I'm being a president. That's what I'm doing. And I think it's time for you to head up to your room," Lauren whispered.

"I think not! It's just Thursday night. I don't have any intake, so I think I'll sit down here and have some fun for a bit longer." Janelle hopped off the bar stool, snatched up her heels, grabbed her half-empty drink, and stumbled toward the stud. Lauren lingered long enough to see the stud put her hand on Janelle. *I don't have time for this. It's been two months since we ended things. She is the worst one yet. FUCK!*

Chapter 2

The knock at the door woke Lauren from her cat nap. She'd already had two meetings with her sorority board and was exhausted, but she knew sleeping at these sorority events was rare, so she stole every minute she could. She slid off the bed and stabilized herself on the wall. Damn, she was tired.

"Here I come," she yelled at the hotel door. She put on her rainbow tie-dye Crocs and opened her hotel room door. "Yes?"

"Well, Ms. President," Jessica said, licking her lips as she inhaled Lauren's beautiful body. Lauren completely forgot she slipped out of her dress before her nap. She quickly disappeared from the hotel door and allowed it to close, but Jessica stopped it with her foot. Lauren returned with a plush white robe with the hotel's gold monogram stitched on the chest wrapped around her body.

"How can I help you, Jessica?" Lauren smirked.

"You can rewind for about 45 seconds and never pick up your robe," Jessica looked Lauren up and down as if the robe didn't exist.

"Is this why you are at my room door," Lauren opened her robe and propped it behind her hands on her hips. Her pale pink lace thongs stretched across her hips while her small C-cup breasts were untamed. "Well, is it?"

The hotel hallways were empty, and most sisters took the chance to rest before they were on duty for the pledges. Jessica's wife, Ambber, was one of the six studs who marched into the hotel lobby earlier that evening and didn't like her being alone with Lauren. Lauren never stopped her from making a move, but she wasn't willing to risk her marriage.

"No, it isn't, but I may be able to add it to my agenda," Jessica pressed her body against Lauren's, pushing past the door and into the hotel room. Before the door could close, Lauren caught it and held it open.

"What was on your agenda?" Lauren was annoyed; she knew this was a waste of time and had about ten minutes before Tiffany arrived for their meeting.

"We need to run down the pledge schedule for the weekend," she rolled her eyes; one of these days, she would find out why everyone lost their mind about Lauren but not at an event.

"Ok, you have seven minutes," Lauren closed her robe and sat on the couch near her bed. There was no need to let Jessica sit on her bed if she'd never lay in it with her. The two ran over the itinerary separated into dates, times, and color codes on the printout in their hands. Lauren made changes where she felt necessary, and Jessica took notes, making sure not to miss any of the adjustments. The conversation started to slow down about five minutes later.

"Looks like you made your time limit. Thanks for coming down. I'll see you with the pledges in the lobby at nine." Lauren tightened her robe, her signal to get out.

"Thanks, I'll see you later," Jessica quickly exited the room only to meet Tiffany on the other side of the door. "Oh, you're her next appointment. Hmph. Figures."

"Hi, sis and you know better," Tiffany laughed Jessica off to avoid misunderstanding. She couldn't afford any of these women to start a rumor about her.

"Don't be inappropriate, Jessica. Goodbye." Lauren waved her off after appearing in the doorway, looking miraculously exactly as she had earlier that evening with her dress and shoes in place. "Come in, Tiffany."

Jessica rolled her eyes at Tiffany before speed-walking down the hallway. Tiffany closed the hotel room door and turned her attention to Lauren.

"You're just in time. I just ran through intake with the Membership Director, and I have some slight adjustments for our itinerary." Lauren picked up the printout with all of Jessica's notes; she'd taken a picture of it with her phone before leaving the original copy with Lauren. She started reading the changes off the paper and giving Tiffany notes to add to her itinerary.

"Is that all?" she asked once Lauren lowered the paper and quieted.

"I think so; if I think of anything else, I will text you," Lauren responded. The two were sitting on the edge of Lauren's bed, and Lauren leaned into Tiffany. "Is everything okay with you?"

"Yes, President Jacobson. The convention is always stressful, as you know, but I'm good. This isn't new for me." Tiffany stood up, putting distance between her and Lauren. She checked her phone, "Wow, I've been up here for 20 minutes already. I gotta get back to my room and get changed for my date."

"I'll see you later. Just close my door on the way out," Lauren started rummaging through her suitcase, disinterested in anything else Tiffany had to say. This hard-to-get thing Tiffany was doing was getting annoying.

Lauren quickly changed into pink and black cotton shorts and a peekaboo belly tank top with sorority letters across her back. She pulled one black and one pink ankle sock on her feet and slid them into her rainbow tie-dye Crocs. She touched up in the mirror, grabbed her mini backpack and sorority paddle, and made her way to the lobby by elevator. The ride was quiet, allowing Lauren to sit with her thoughts. She had a lot riding on this weekend with the pledges, but more importantly, she had plans with someone special Saturday night. They'd planned this for the last two months; she was just two days away.

"Innnnnnnnncorporated!" Four sorors yelled as the elevator doors opened. They quickly hid their liquor bottles behind their backs and got out of Lauren's sight.

"Every fucking time," Lauren whispered. She was tired of the younger ones thinking her events were weekend-long club visits to get drunk and sleep around. The least they could do was hide it better.

"Well, well, well. You all actually look like you may have a chance to...what the hell is that?" A line of 14 women stood before Lauren dressed in all-black biking shorts, black hoodies, and black sneakers, moving and speaking in unison. Her attention was directed at the second to last woman to her left wearing white socks, the only one wearing white socks. Lauren was suddenly in front of the young woman and surprised her with a slap of her sorority paddle across the woman's calf, causing her knee to buckle, but she quickly regained her balance. "WHITE SOCKS! Did y'all get the requirements for this night?"

All 14 women yelled in unison, "Yes, Big Sister RoYal PHlush!"

"Then why the hell do I see white socks on my line!" Lauren responded, swinging her paddle, signaling her sisters to respond to the intake, "It seems there is a very weak link."

Sorors rushed to surround the young, light-skinned, thin woman wearing white socks, yelling at her so close she could feel and smell every single one of their breaths. The rest of the intake line answered every question Lauren asked in unison without fail. The white socks were quickly pushed off the young woman's feet before she returned her shoes to her bare feet. The sorors backed off her as she stood up.

"Eh, no one saw these white socks on their line sister?" Lauren scanned the line for a response and was met with silence. "Oh, so y'all are individuals, right? Y'all not on line...you don't have line sisters...you aren't one?"

The white socks intake stepped forward out the line, "Permission to speak Big Sister RoYal PHlush?"

"I shouldn't let you say anything. Go ahead," Lauren waved the young woman off, allowing her to speak.

"Please don't blame my line sisters; they have been more than supportive during this process. I will take the punishment for all 13 of my line sisters." She stood separated from her line but still standing identical to them, eyes straight forward, making sure not to look at anyone.

Lauren pointed her paddle at the woman's face, just an inch away from touching her nose. "You all actually look like you may have a chance to be a member of MY organization! Now get your ass back in line, and don't step out my line again."

The young woman stepped back into line without looking at her line sisters. The sorors continued to quiz the pledges, yelling questions from their manual, something they should've known verbatim. It didn't take long for them to wear out their welcome in the hotel lobby, and they would have to move to another location.

"Alright, it's time to take this outside!" Nicole stood at the end of the intake line and directed the intake to the front of the hotel. "Let's get moving! We have a long night ahead of us."

The women rushed outside together while reciting a sorority poem. The next 5 hours were filled with yelling, repeating sorority information, and pushing the intake to physical exertion. By 2 am, Lauren realized she was two hours late for her date. She was sure her tardiness wouldn't detour things, but she didn't want to push it further. The second group of sorors arrived to take over the intake night. They split the night to make sure the sorors were energized to keep pushing the pledges.

"Ladies! It's our turn!" Jessica yelled, walking down the sidewalk towards the group of women. Six sisters followed behind her, chanting and yelling. She nodded at Lauren as she passed her, "President Jacobson."

"Jessica," Lauren didn't bother looking at her. She knew she was only irritated because she wasn't lucky enough to know how Lauren's bed felt. "Level one! Time to go. Let level two get started.

LAUREN QUICKLY APPROACHED her hotel room door; she needed this chance to relax before Friday's activities started. She stood in front of the door, closed her eyes, and took a deep breath. Focusing on slowing her breathing and heart rate, she didn't want to give Kelsey the impression that she was excited to see her.

She pushed open the door and was met by the aroma of tropical sweet fruit-scented candles. Kelsey had positioned her chocolate curves across the white linen before falling asleep waiting for her. Lauren tickled her thighs but didn't get a response, not even to shake her off. She didn't have time to do this the sensual way, she smacked Kelsey's bare ass cheek, and she jerked awake.

"Fuck you, Ren, fuck you!" Kelsey yelled when she realized the smack came from Lauren towering over her in the bed.

"I plan to fuck you," Lauren smiled and pulled Kelsey to the edge of the bed. Kelsey wanted to give her an attitude, but she was too afraid Lauren would send her away and invite someone else to her room. Instead, she positioned her soft, full ass on the edge of the bed, spread her legs, and pressed her knees to her chest. Lauren was presented with a perfect view of Kelsey's shaven, wet, pulsating mound. She acted like she didn't like to be spanked, but her cum running down her ass told a different story.

"Well, what the hell are you waiting for? She's not going to eat herself," Kelsey said impatiently, smirking. Lauren smacked her ass again and watched the wave move from one cheek to the other. Kelsey moaned softly and apologized in silence.

"Don't fuck with me tonight, Kelsey, I'll leave you like this until the morning," Lauren scolded. She kneeled and positioned her face just above Kelsey's thighs. She gently kissed Kelsey, followed by her tongue running between her lips. She rocked her body on Lauren's tongue while she licked and sucked and slid her tongue inside her. Moans grew louder, breathing deeper. She was close. Kelsey let out a loud moan and clamped her thighs around her head.

After Kelsey's orgasm subsided, Lauren pulled herself closer, sliding two fingers into her.

"Oh shit," Kelsey gasped. Lauren continued to lick as she slowly stroked her with her fingers. Kelsey's breathing quickened, signaling Lauren to go faster. "Oh fuck!"

Kelsey barely held onto her legs as she came, squirting. She looked down at Lauren with concern. She'd never done that before. Lauren chuckled.

"Looks like my job is done," she stood up and wiped her mouth, letting out a small burp. As her mind recovered, she realized she heard a soft, muted bump with voices outside her hotel room door.

"What the hell?" Lauren rushed to the bathroom to grab a towel and wipe her face. Kelsey was still stuck on the bed, putting the noises outside the door far from her mind.

Lauren quickly opened the door to find four sorors standing outside with their eyes full of fear and judgment.

"Hmph, well. What do we have here?" Lauren slowly looked over each soror. Confusion was written across their faces; they didn't know her next move.

"What the hell is this!" Lauren yelled, closing the hotel room door behind her. She placed her foot in the hallway and stepped outside, blocking any escape for the sisters outside.

"We saw Kelsey enter your hotel room late last night, and then you had to leave the intake. We didn't…" The fear of Lauren's consequences rippled through the group as they all stepped back.

Lauren craned her neck and stared at each one of them. "I expect more from you ladies, do you understand? Sneaking around someone's hotel room door is a serious offense. There will be consequences if this ever happens again."

The sorors all nodded in agreement, tension still building in the hallway.

"Now, all of you get out of here before I change up next semester's lineup," Lauren said, her voice reverberating through the hallway.

The sorors scattered and ran away. Lauren sighed as she turned around and stepped back into the hotel room. She knew the girls would keep her secret, which was all that mattered. She had to make sure everyone knew she wasn't someone to be messed with. Lauren looked back at Kelsey and smiled.

"Well, shall we continue?" she said with a sly smirk on her face. She slipped back between Kelsey's legs.

Kelsey looked at her in surprise and said, "Yes, let's."

Chapter 3

Lauren stepped out of the shower the next morning, hoping Kelsey had returned to her room. She didn't want to have that awkward conversation about why they shouldn't be seen together first thing in the morning.

"Kelsey?" Lauren called out into her hotel room. No response. She checked her phone and realized she only had 30 minutes before everyone else would start collecting in the lobby, waiting to board their buses for community service. At every convention, the sorors and bruhs gathered to complete at least four hours of community service. It was a great way to start the pledges out and keep the neophytes honest. This year, they were helping rebuild houses for the displaced. She wore biking shorts, a sports bra, and Nikes to keep it comfortable and cute. Her entire outfit was color-coordinated with pink, turquoise, and white. She rubbed on her smell-good oils and sprayed herself with bug spray before putting the spray in her bag; she knew someone would forget. She headed to the lobby ten minutes early.

"WELL, WELL, LOOK WHO is running behind schedule," Janelle scoffed from a couch in the lobby corner as Lauren exited the elevator.

"I'm right on time, especially since I say what is late." Lauren avoided looking at Janelle and continued scanning the lobby and restaurant for sorors or bruhs. They were the only two in the lobby. She walked over to the couch adjacent to Janelle and leaned on it with her back to her. "Is this going to be a problem?"

"HA!" Janelle walked over to face her. Lauren's disappointment dripped from her expression. Her disgust pierced Janelle's already shattered heart. All her audacity deflated from her body, and Janelle became the fragile woman who loved Lauren so much. She touched Janelle on her shoulder and held her cheek.

Janelle was sobbing uncontrollably. She embraced Lauren tightly, but Lauren didn't allow her to stay in her arms.

"You have to get yourself together," Lauren insisted. She waited for Janelle to gather her thoughts.

Janelle took a deep breath, wiping her tears and mascara from her cheeks. Lauren hated seeing her in this condition, but this shit was getting out of hand. The elevators started opening, releasing floods of sorors and pledges into the hotel lobby. Janelle grabbed Lauren and pulled her into the empty hotel bar.

"I don't have time for this, Janelle," Lauren yanked her hand from her. "We have community service to get to, and the rest of the sisters are coming down now."

Janelle ordered a glass of red wine from the bartender. Lauren stared at her as if she had two heads. The bartender placed the glass in front of Janelle. Janelle reached for it, grabbing Lauren instead of the wine.

Lauren quickly handed the glass to the bartender; she would not make a scene in the hotel bar with all her sisters waiting to board a bus in the lobby. Janelle grabbed her by the waist, pulled her close, and pressed their lips together. She stood there in disbelief as tears rolled down Janelle's cheeks again.

"It's not enough for you to hurt me. Now you have to make me suffer and be humiliated," she sobbed.

"Let go of me now," Lauren struggled to free herself from Janelle's embrace. She turned and looked into the hotel bar mirror to see who was paying attention to them. No one seemed to be.

"You know I love you," Janelle continued. "I will always love you. Please don't leave me," she fell to her knees in front of Lauren. Lauren rolled her eyes and turned her back to her. She hated this type of melodrama.

Lauren reached into her bag, pulled out her sorority paddle, and nudged her with it. Janelle cowered, putting her hands over her head, expecting a hit. Lauren grabbed her by her hair and pulled her up. She whispered in her ear, "If you ever make a scene like this in public again, I will fuck you up. Do you understand?"

Janelle nodded and walked back towards the lobby, with Lauren following her.

"I expect you to keep this weekend's events discreet. There are sorors and bruhs everywhere, and they don't know about you and me," Lauren whispered behind Janelle. "You are done. We are done, and we aren't doing this again."

Janelle watched Lauren walk past her and disappear into the sea of women. Her eyes swelled up with tears again, but they were dry before they fell. She'd be the bigger person and let this go. Lauren's heart was so black to Janelle, and she'd never change her ways.

LAUREN WATCHED FROM the front of the bus as the members and pledges made their way to the community service house.

"We will be here for four hours. The work is divided into teams of 4. Tiffany will select the groups and assign your duties," Lauren informed the other sorors. "I don't want any problems today. We are here to sweat, so let's get started."

After just under four hours of moving soil from one pile to the other and wheeling the dirt in the back of pickup trucks, Lauren sat down for a quick break.

"Oh, don't look so bored," Nicole said, checking out her sports bra and shorts that were soiled with dirt stains worn like a badge. "We are just about done, and you can get out of all this dirt and take a nice hot shower."

Lauren looked around and saw everyone was busy moving soil and collecting debris. No one had time to stop and stare at the president. She decided not to engage with Nicole. Her best behavior was a requirement with Nicole around. She didn't hold a position in the sorority, but her wife was the president of the Bruhs fraternity. She was the only woman Lauren knew could rival her status. It would be her first convention with Nicole. Lauren had too much going on with Kelsey, Janelle, and the sorors lingering at her hotel room door to get comfortable.

"How are the bruhs doing?" Lauren asked as she wiped her hands on the back of her shorts. She hoped a distraction would work to stop her from thinking about all the shit she'd let happen this weekend.

Nicole smiled, "They are doing great. I don't think any of them will let us down."

"That's what I like to hear."

The two sat together quietly until a bus pulled up. The women returned to the buses to head back to the hotel. As they rode, Lauren looked out the window at the beautiful views of Miami Beach, thinking about her plans for Saturday night. She fantasized about her lover's tongue. A pulse started between her thighs; she wondered how long they would last. Her mind raced with her touches. She didn't know what she wanted from her, but her body was already craving her touch. She could barely focus on the things around her. She rubbed her thighs together, hoping to get some relief before returning to the hotel. She noticed Nicole glance at her occasionally.

As soon as the bus reached a complete stop in front of the hotel, Lauren jumped off. She walked through the lobby and towards her room as fast as possible. She avoided any conversations. She could barely contain herself. Her door opened before she could use her keycard, and she was quickly pulled inside.

"Oh shit!" Lauren yelled as she fell into the hotel room. Kelsey immediately closed the door, locked it, and pushed her into the wall.

"I know you were thinking about me," she smirked as she pressed her body into Lauren.

"Did you go to community service? How did you get up here so fast?" Lauren questioned, pushing Kelsey away. "What the fuck are you doing here? Someone could have seen you."

Kelsey looked at Lauren in disappointment. She was about to tell Lauren how badly she needed her when Lauren looked away, grabbed her phone and earbuds, and began to listen to music.

"Lauren," Kelsey didn't want to wait anymore for her. She pulled Lauren's phone out of her hand and dropped it to the floor. She grabbed Lauren by her hair and kissed her neck, causing a slight smile to creep on her face. Kelsey attacked her neck, nibbling and biting. Lauren admitted she was turned on but didn't want Kelsey right now. And this was not the way she'd go about it.

Kelsey kissed Lauren's chest and grabbed her breasts. She wanted to hear her moans, she wanted her to beg, and she wanted her to submit to her. Lauren closed her eyes and enjoyed the attention. Kelsey reached for Lauren's shorts, pulling them down. Lauren quickly opened her eyes and wrapped her fingers around her throat.

"What do you think this is?" Lauren demanded, increasing the pressure around her neck. No answer. She reached into Kelsey's shorts and ripped off her thongs.

Kelsey gasped; her eyes widened as Lauren grabbed her wrists and pinned them above her head against the wall.

"Don't move your hands," Lauren commanded. She released Kelsey's wrists. Kelsey didn't move. She wasn't sure what to do, but she complied. Lauren was starting to scare her. "Why are you playing with me?"

Kelsey didn't respond. She couldn't. Fingers maintained their pressure on her neck. Tears fell from her eyes.

"You. Need. Me. I don't need you. You come when I call for you. Do you understand?" Kelsey shook her head yes.

Lauren reached between her thighs and aggressively stroked her. Kelsey's eyes rolled, leaning her neck into her hand, needing Lauren to squeeze tighter as her fingers invaded her.

"Fuck, fuck, fuck!" Kelsey whispered. She couldn't move with Lauren still choking and fingering her, but she felt like she would jump out of her skin. She raised her leg over Lauren's shoulder and rode her fingers deeper and deeper until she came. Lauren released her neck, and she fell to the floor. She looked up. Lauren pointed towards the bathroom. Kelsey took the direction and stumbled to stand.

"Get yourself together in there and get the fuck out of my room. Don't do this shit again," Lauren tossed Kelsey's ripped panties on her before slamming the bathroom door behind her.

"FUCK!" Lauren yelled, punching the pillows on her bed. She lay on the bed staring at the ceiling while she calmed down. She didn't have much time. "Fucking Probate."

After hearing Kelsey leave her hotel room, Lauren realized she had a meeting with Nu Delta Xi before probate. She collected herself and her laptop bag and scanned the room before heading out of her hotel room. She'd definitely need a nap after this meeting before probate.

THE INCESSANT RINGING of her phone woke her. She reached blindly and followed the vibrations on her bed. It was Kelsey. "What!"

"I'm sorry, Ren. I didn't mean to…I know I fucked up," Kelsey started. Lauren heard her sniffling through the phone.

"I don't know what you want me to say. You know where I stand," Lauren responded. She didn't know what more she expected from her, but she knew this nap was over.

"I don't know why I do this shit, but please don't be mad. I'm sorry, okay?" Kelsey begged.

"I'm not mad. I don't know how many times I can say this. We aren't together. We fuck around from time to time, but you can't seem to get that," Lauren paused, "I'm done with you."

"Ren, I'm sorry," Kelsey pleaded. She knew it was a waste of time but couldn't help herself.

"Yeah. I don't want to play these fucking games anymore. You need to move on," Lauren responded.

"What if I can't? What if I need you? What if I love you?" she lingered on the silent air.

"Don't bullshit me. You don't love me. You love my tongue. You love how I make your body feel, but you don't love me," Lauren responded honestly. Kelsey said nothing, and Lauren hung up the phone.

Everyone she messed with said they loved her. They didn't even know her. They loved to be dominated by a feminine woman. They loved the idea of her…but didn't give a fuck about her for real. She was sure Saturday would change all that.

Chapter 4

Lauren jumped out of bed, showered, put on her Nu Nu Lambda tee shirt, denim shorts, and sneakers, and walked out the door.

Today was the day that all new members of Nu Nu Lambda Sorority, Inc. were introduced to the sorority during their Probate Show. Lauren worked hard with the new members and was excited about their performance. She smiled as she walked towards the hotel ballroom, thinking about how far they had come since they started rehearsals months ago.

When she reached the room, it was buzzing with energy from all the sorors and bruhs who came to support the new members. Lauren spotted Kelsey in line, waiting to be checked in by her sorors. She felt a familiar urge to go over and talk for a moment but quickly squashed it.

As the lights dimmed and the music began, Lauren proudly watched her sisters take the stage and perform their hearts out. When it came time for them to welcome in the new members, Lauren and the other newbies were taken by all their sorors' love and support. They glowed with pride as they showcased their hard work and talents.

"Introducing the Summer 2024 line of Nu Nu Lambda Sorority, Innnnnnnnncorporated: Nu Amore," Lauren said as she gleamed with pride. The sorors stormed the stage, hugging their new sisters, throwing up their hand signs, and yelling out their call. As the ladies calmed down, they started exiting the stage.

"RoYal PHlush!" a younger, brown-skinned woman with long blonde curly hair wearing light blue jeggings, a fitted sorority t-shirt, and matching Jordans yelled. Lauren turned to see baby sis Sammie waving at her through the crowd.

"Are you just getting here?" Lauren asked Sammie as she hugged her.

"I mean, it's not like y'all needed me yesterday. I can't handle intake yet." Sammie smiled slyly, knowing that wasn't a good enough answer.

"So, the President's baby sister doesn't come to the pledge night or community service, and I'm supposed to be okay with that?" Lauren crossed her arms. "I don't think so."

"Will you spend the rest of the night scolding me, or will you have some fun? It's not like I can change it now." Sammie laughed. Lauren rolled her eyes and pulled her in for another hug.

"Who'd you take down already?" Sammie whispered in her ear. She pulled back from their embrace and chuckled. Sammie was the only one there who knew Lauren... who truly loved her.

"You talk too damn much, sis," Lauren pushed Sammie towards the bar. "Let's get a drink."

The two women walked through the crowd, using small talk and each other to avoid deeper conversations with others. They reached the bar, and Lauren ordered two whiskey sours and invited Sammie to sit with her. They caught up with each other.

Sammie was completing her second master's degree and working with a nonprofit helping entrepreneurs. Lauren talked about finishing her master's degree and focusing on the sorority.

"Do you work?" Sammie laughed.

"Yes, don't act like that," Lauren responded.

"I'm just saying. I have never heard of you working a job," Sammie leaned in. Lauren smacked Sammie's thigh and laughed.

The crowd started cheering and rushing towards the stage. Boots thudding against the ground echoed through the conference room, silencing conversations and redirecting their attention to the bruhs gathering on the stage.

"Damn, she fine!" the sisters cheered. Eight masculine-dressed lesbian studs stepped in unison. They recited fraternity poems and chants. A caramel-complexioned stud dressed in her fraternity paraphernalia stood in the middle of the stage, shining her beautiful smile on the crowd.

"Y'all know we only bring the best of the best. I already hear you ladies drooling over them," she laughed, and the women cheered in agreeance. Before announcing their line name, she continued introducing each new bruh by their new fraternal name. They lined up together, "Introducing, Catalytic, the Summer 2024 line of Nu Delta Xi Fraternity, Incorporated."

The room was filled with celebration and applause. Bruhs rushed the stage, dapped their new bruhs, shouted their call, and threw up their hand signs. The stage slowly cleared as the DJ started playing music. The new family danced, drank, and got to know each other.

As Lauren swayed to the music with her champagne glass hanging above her head, she felt something approaching. She opened her eyes, and a light-skinned, tall stud with hazel eyes and dark glistening waves parted the crowd towards her. Annoyance rose inside her.

"Lauren," the stud greeted her.

"El, what can I do for you?" Lauren responded and continued to sway to the music.

"You know I don't go by El anymore. Just call me MelindaTivatN or Melinda." KapTivatN was the president of Nu Delta Xi Fraternity and Nicole's wife.

"Kap, what can I do for you?" Lauren rolled her eyes and sipped her champagne.

"We need to set up some time tomorrow morning to speak about one of your members," Melinda leaned in and whispered into Lauren's ear. "She's creating waves."

Lauren's swaying abruptly stopped. She made direct eye contact with Melinda and responded, "9 am in my room. You know my room number, right?"

"I'll see you at nine." Melinda quickly turned and walked away. She searched for Nicole in the crowd. She wrapped her arms around her waist, and they lost themselves in each other.

Fuck, fuck, fuck! Is she talking about Janelle? Was Janelle with anyone other than PHenox this weekend? And if it wasn't Janelle, who was Melinda talking about? Lauren sat her champagne glass on the first table she passed as she exited the party. Sammie watched Lauren talking to Melinda and followed her out.

"What the fuck is going on?" Sammie whispered.

Lauren jumped and quickly collected herself, "Nothing, just some NDX drama. You know they have to report everything to me."

"Cuz you the boss!" Sammie reluctantly laughed and high-fived Lauren. *This bitch really thinks she is fooling me.* "Then why are you out here?"

"I just needed some air. It was getting thick in there. I hate being the party pooper, so I'll come out here and let them have their fun," Lauren lied. "I'm heading back to my room. Are you coming?"

Sammie stepped back and read Lauren's face. Her seductive grin let Sammie know what to expect next. "Mmmm, yep."

The two women continued chatting while walking to the elevator.

The party's vibe shifted. The DJ played slow jams, hips swayed, hands explored, and people slowly exited the ballroom.

"Are you ready for the next party?" Brittani asked Janelle. Her arms were wrapped around Brittani's neck, their bodies pressed together, dancing in unison.

"There's another party?" Janelle whispered. She looked at her sorors dancing with each other and bruhs. Two bruhs were at a corner table kissing or whispering to each other. *I wonder if anyone else sees this?*

"A few of us are moving this to Aaron's room," she responded. Janelle held her hand as they walked off the dance floor and settled at a table.

"Who is Aaron?" Janelle asked.

"Oh, damn. I mean Virile," Brittani laughed.

"Mmmm, this is going to be fun." *That's who I saw in the corner. Who was with her? Damn, they are gone already.*

The ballroom was bare, with just the DJ closing and a couple of women cleaning up. Brittani jumped up, twirled her around, and pulled her towards the door.

"HAVE YOU EVER BEEN to one of our after-parties?" Brittani pulled Janelle closer as they rode the elevator.

"No, this is my first National Convention," she rocked her hips, pressing her butt against Brittani's dildo tucked in her pants. "So, you're going to need that at this after-party?"

"You have no idea," she smirked. The elevator door opened to music echoing down the hallway. Brittani wrapped her arm around Janelle's neck and pulled her in for a kiss. The music grew louder as they walked down the hallway. They halted in front of a door vibrating from the bass moving through it. "At any point, you can say no, and if it becomes too much, we can go back to my room. Are you ready?"

Say no to what? How could a hotel party be so much? If she's wearing her strap-on, then this must be some sort of sex party, right? "As ready as I will ever be," Janelle smiled nervously.

Brittani knocked on the door four times rapidly, then two slow and three more rapid knocks. She looked down at Janelle and smiled reassuringly. The hotel door opened slightly with the latch still secured. A tall chocolate sculpted topless stud peeked out.

"Aye, PHenox, I didn't think you'd make it," the stud smiled.

"Come on now, Virile, you know I can't miss one of your parties. Are you going to open the door?" she knocked softly on the door.

"Who is this?" Virile frowned at Janelle.

"This my bae, Janelle. She's a neo, but she's good." She vouched for Janelle, but Virile didn't seem to believe her. She darted her eyes between the two of them. Brittani offered, "She's in the deck."

"Oh, why didn't you say that!" Virile laughed and unlatched the door. Her entire body looked like someone took years to build; she stood proudly wearing only her boxer briefs stuffed with her strap-on. "Verbal non-disclosure. Everything you see and do here stays here. We protect each other like family. Cool?"

"I got it, but what is in the deck?" Janelle asked but was ignored. The suite was lit with colorful LED lights and small candles. Two queen beds in the bedroom and a pull-out couch in the living room were covered with naked women. Virile pointed towards two bowls on the table filled with dental dam and condoms, liquor in the cabinet and refrigerator, and feminine wipes and body wash in the bathroom. *So, nobody heard me, huh?*

"Have fun," Virile kissed Brittani on the lips. "Come find me later."

"What is in the deck?" Janelle smacked Brittani's arm.

"Damn," Brittani grabbed her hand, laughing. "It just means you messed with Lauren."

"How does in the deck mean messing with Lauren? Why is it okay for you to tell people that?" Janelle pulled away from her. She quickly pulled Janelle into her, cupping her face in her hand.

"Bae, chill out. You're new, so you don't know 'bout Lauren. She likes to mess with the neos. She probably slept with half of Nu Nu Lambda. Her line name is a card game term, so the bruhs say all the women she's messed with are in the deck of cards," Brittani explained.

"And that is an automatic entry into this," Janelle looked around the hotel suite. Two bruhs and one soror caught her attention. *Damn.*

"It just means you must be discrete if Lauren chose you, so you're safe with us," Brittani finished. She pulled Janelle into the suite. They stopped for a drink and took off their shirts and shoes. Leaning against the counter with Janelle pressed against her, Brittani eyed Virile in the bedroom, hovering over a stud bent over in front of her. She looked up at Brittani and smiled. Brittani didn't look away. She nodded towards the bed and raised her eyebrow, waiting for an answer. Brittani flicked her finger at a woman in the living room, and she walked towards them. She gave Virile the signal to wait a moment.

"Oh my...shit!" Janelle leaned forward, enjoying Nicole's lips on her nipples. She removed the rest of her clothes, complying with Nicole's every silent demand. *Where'd Brittani go? Shit, Nicole's fingers, her tongue, shit.*

LAUREN LED SAMMIE TO her hotel room. Once inside, Lauren ran her fingers through Sammie's curls and tightened her grip on her hair. Sammie released a soft moan, relaxing her body against Lauren's, and kicked off her Jordans.

"Off," Lauren whispered and released Sammie's hair. Sammie quickly complied by peeling off her jeggings and pulling her t-shirt over her head. She was naked from the waist down, no panties or hair. A pink and black Victoria's Secret lace bra fell down her arms, freeing her small, chocolate-drop breasts. She didn't move, only waited for Lauren's next instruction. "Get on your knees."

Sammie kneeled before Lauren and watched her lower her shorts to the floor. She lifted her leg, putting Sammie face to face with her hairless invitation. She wrapped her fingers in Sammie's hair and pulled her in. Sammie licked and sucked her, eager to please her. She rode Sammie's tongue to two orgasms. She released Sammie and fell back onto the bed. Sammie grabbed her clothes and went into the bathroom to clean herself up. Lauren listened as small moans came from the bathroom until Sammie let out a loud, "Oh fuck". Five minutes later, Sammie emerged from the bathroom, perfectly dressed, and smiled at Lauren sitting on the bed, fully clothed, swiping through her phone.

"So, what's up with you and the baby bruh?" Lauren laughed.

"Don't play me, sis. You know PHenox is my bae. We're not together or anything, but she's fun. Why?" Sammie knew Lauren was on some messiness.

"She was in the hotel bar Thursday night with Janelle. Rubbing all on her lil fatty in front of the other bruhs," Lauren kept her eyes locked on her phone, continuing to swipe.

She fell on the bed next to Lauren. "Good for her because Janelle has a nice fat ass, and if she didn't, I probably would."

Lauren shot Sammie a dagger stare but quickly softened and chuckled, "You're funny."

"Shit, let me get back to my room. I have a date tonight with PHenox," she jumped up, dancing across the room.

"Make sure you are protecting yourself," Lauren laughed.

"From what? You?" She licked her lips, "I think that ship has sailed, don't you?"

"No, from the other pussies sitting on PHenox's face," Lauren responded. "Now it's time for you to go. It's almost midnight. I have a long day tomorrow."

"And I have a face to sit on," Sammie headed towards the door. She kissed Lauren on the lips. "Bye, sis."

"Love you, bye," Lauren closed her hotel room door. She leaned against it and ran her hands across her body, caressing her nipples, inner thighs, and neck. She was still horny but shook it off, took a deep breath, and started going through her clothes. Tomorrow morning, she had a meeting with Melinda. She still hadn't figured out who she was talking about. Then, the family outing most of the day. After that, the club and her night to herself and her boo. Sunday morning was closing the event, goodbyes, then to the airport. She pulled off her clothes and underwear and stuffed them into the dirty clothes side of her suitcase before stuffing it back into the closet. She grabbed a towel and turned on the shower.

Chapter 5

Lauren was having breakfast when Melinda knocked on her hotel room door the next morning. "Come in."

"Good morning," she sat down next to Lauren. "How's your morning?"

"Let's get to it, Melinda," Lauren hurried her along.

"Ok, right to it. Well, it's Kelsey," Melinda sighed. "She's getting around."

"What the hell does that mean, Melinda? Are your bois getting their panties in a bunch over her?" Lauren made fun of the bruhs but knew Kelsey had been needy over the last few months, and she wasn't getting the added attention from Lauren, so it had to come from somewhere.

"They can handle her, but she's getting a reputation. I don't want any of your ladies to have that look with my org, but I can't make them stop sleeping with her. Is there anything you can do?" she asked.

"Why do I have to do anything? It's okay for the bruhs to sleep with her knowing all the other bruhs she's been with, but then they want to talk shit about her because they are all choosing to sleep with her one right after the other?" Lauren smirked. "Does that make sense to you?"

"That's a, no?" Melinda asked.

"If you can't stop them from sleeping with her, what makes you think I can stop her from sleeping with them? Technically, she isn't doing anything wrong. It's not getting in the way of official business, right?" Lauren leaned in.

"Right," Melinda reluctantly agreed.

"Explain to me what we are discussing again. We should be discussing your bruhs verbal abuse towards Kelsey. The way we speak about our family members is in the bylaws. So, what are you going to do about that?" Lauren knew Melinda didn't want that response, but with everything going on with her and Kelsey, talking to her about the bruhs she was sleeping with was the last thing she wanted to do.

"I have a meeting planned for next week once everyone is settled in back home," Melinda reassured Lauren.

"Great, well, it looks like you have everything under control. Thank you for taking the time to come to me with your concerns. My door is always open if you ever need help with your role as president again." Lauren walked her to the door. "I'll see you in the city today."

"See you soon," she said, shaking her head and starting down the hotel hallway. It always took her off guard when she talked to Lauren. *How she could turn any situation in her favor was mind-boggling.*

Lauren sat back down to finish her breakfast. She was pleased with how she handled the situation. She was sure this would become something more, but it didn't. She quickly cleaned up and headed to the hotel lobby to meet everyone else for their family outing.

"MA'AM, HERE ARE YOUR tags for your chairs and umbrellas. Is there anything else we can do for you?" the sun reflected off the black waves of this dark-skinned young man.

"No, that's all. Thank you." Lauren tossed a few dollars in the tip jar the young man kept looking at. She walked towards the group of chairs and umbrellas she rented for the sorors. She counted them off individually as the sorors put their claim on them.

"Enjoy yourself, ladies!" Lauren yelled to her group of sorors. They rushed to find their beach home for the rest of the day, some with chairs leaned back, allowing the sun to kiss their skin, others shielding themselves under umbrellas. Janelle and Nicole lay on giant blankets between two beach chairs and umbrellas, reading their books and pushing glasses back up their noses. Brittani stretched towards the sand and caught Janelle's attention.

"You better quit playing with me," Janelle giggled, pressing the palm of her hand into Brittani's bare chest. "You will get me in trouble."

"Why?" Brittani whispered.

"Because we are at an event. It's enough that I'm over here in y'all area. This isn't even a part of the sorors' chairs and umbrellas," she complained. "I just don't need any more shit."

"I got you; you know that right?" Brittani pressed her body weight against her hand. "You're my responsibility now."

Janelle was enveloped by Brittani's aura, leaning in for more. Their lips softly touched enough to shield their dancing tongues. Janelle fell into her. She pressed her fingertips into Janelle's wrist, and her hand slipped onto the blanket.

"Let's remember where we are while we are having fun!" Lauren yelled before walking past Janelle and Brittani. Janelle's soft, affectionate demeanor stiffened.

"See," Janelle's eyes darted down at the ground. Brittani kissed her forehead, then her cheek, and she softened onto the blanket. Brittani laid back on the chair after shooting a glare at Lauren. The sun peaked on the side of her umbrella and warmed her body, wearing only a small black bikini. Her long black locs fell off the chair as she closed her eyes. With each breath she took, she sank into the chair.

Lauren stopped just out of their view, exchanged pleasantries with Melinda, and made her way to her chair. She released her bikini cover across her chair and propped her legs up.

"Are you ok?" Melinda asked Janelle.

"Huh," she smirked shyly. "Yeah, I'm good."

"I'm here for you if you need to talk," Melinda reassured her with a smile.

"Is that all you are available for?" she playfully teased but leaned away when Melinda stretched towards her.

"When you're ready," Melinda laughed. She hung her head, but Melinda responded, "It's ok. When you're ready."

She smiled at Melinda and held Nicole's hand. The two continued reading their books.

THE SORORS AND BRUHS spent the afternoon on the beach. They played like children in the sand, splashing each other in the sea. They ate from the local food trucks and enjoyed the Miami sun. They ventured up and down the strip, buying souvenirs and drinks. After a few hours, they settled down, resting on the beach again.

Sammie splashed playfully as she ran out of the ocean. She swung her towel across her shoulders and caught a glimpse of Brittani handing Janelle a bottle of water. Janelle's sweet smile and Brittani's attentiveness made Sammie nauseous. *What was so special about Janelle? Why was Brittani so into her?*

"Hey babe," Sammie yelled. She waited for Brittani to look away from Janelle. Without a response, Sammie made her way to their chairs. "You don't hear me sexy?"

"Oh, shit, Sammie, I'm sorry, girl. I didn't hear you. I was talking," she smiled at Janelle, blushing.

"I see, but that means you don't see me?" She asked.

"Don't do that, Sammie. When I'm with you, I'm focused on only you. Same when I'm with Janelle," Brittani's brows wrinkled.

"That only works when I'm not around," Sammie laughed.

"We'll talk more tonight at the hotel. Have fun," she said, blowing Sammie a kiss and returning her attention to Janelle. Sammie rolled her eyes and walked away.

"Lauren, babe! Let's get some time in the water before it gets too dark," Sammie said, smiling.

"Girl, I'm done with the water. We are here for another hour, and the bus will be back to pick us up," Lauren said as she turned over onto her stomach and released the straps on her swim top. "Now grab that sunscreen and put more on my back so I can even this tan out for tonight."

"Ugh! Fine." Sammie threw her body into the beach chair beside Lauren and sprayed the lotion on Lauren's back before massaging it.

Nicole lay asleep topless, sweat beading on her back and her book still cradled in her hands. The sun seemed tired as it sank out of the sky. The umbrella shielded the four of them. Janelle giggled at Brittani playfully tugging at her swimsuit. She softly swatted her hands. Janelle's lips met Brittani's, and she inhaled her breath. Brittani gasped from the chill that slid under her bikini top. She peaked at a hand with a tattoo stretching across the light caramel wrist, letting her know it was Melinda's hand. Melinda stroked her nipple, combined with Janelle's sweet kisses, and the heat grew between her legs. Nicole groaned, waking up to Melinda pressing against her back. She caressed Janelle's thigh, tracing her suit bottom.

"Ladies, the bus will be here in 30 minutes, so please make sure to clean up after yourself and be ready on the sidewalk," Lauren announced to the sorority and fraternity spread across the beach.

Brittani was startled and disappointed. Janelle quickly closed her legs and pulled away from her. Nicole kissed the back of Janelle's neck reassuringly.

"Let's get our stuff together so we can get out of here," Melinda said. She rubbed Nicole's shoulder, calming her. They were sure that the announcement was meant to interrupt. "We need to get ready for the club tonight anyway. Y'all ready to have a good time tonight?"

"I am going to enjoy dancing," Janelle laughed.

"Save me a dance?" Nicole asked.

"Of course," Janelle blushed.

"Only if you can get her away from me," Brittani hugged her.

"Yeah, yeah, yeah. There's going to be a lot of people at the club tonight, so I'm sure she'll have some time to roam," Melinda winked at Brittani while folding their belongings.

Chapter 6

"Are you ready to see me tonight?" Lauren whispered into her phone as she lay across her hotel bed. "Mmmm, really. I can't wait to see what it is."

She wrapped up her phone call and finished getting dressed for the club. *Okay, so I'll stay for maybe two hours, then make my way to Bae. Everyone will be too lit by then to notice me leaving.* Lauren checked out her pale pink dress that stopped right below her butt in the mirror. The dress was sleeveless with a high neckline, drawing all eyes on her legs. *Perfect.* She checked her phone. She had 26 minutes before everyone had to be in the lobby. *I'll head down 15 minutes early to catch a drink at the bar.* A knock at the door. Lauren threw on her robe and answered it.

"Hey, babe," Kelsey said, smiling.

"What do you want?" Lauren responded. Kelsey reached for Lauren's hand, but she wrapped her hands behind her back. "Kelsey, what is it?"

"I just wanted to apologize again. We can fix this," she pleaded.

"No, we can't. It's done. I'm done. You need to stop this and move on. Shit, why can't y'all get it?" Lauren sighed.

"Y'all? Who else are you fucking?" Kelsey asked angrily.

"That's none of your business. I need to finish getting dressed. I'll see you downstairs." Lauren slammed the door. She waited for a moment just in case Kelsey decided to knock again, but nothing. She finished the last touches on her makeup and another knock at the door. *Fuck! Kelsey is going to make me lose it on her.*

"What are you not getting!" Lauren yelled as she opened the door, startling Janelle.

"I didn't...I'm sorry," Janelle stammered.

"Shit. I thought you were someone else. I'm sorry. What's up?" Lauren opened the door, welcoming Janelle into her room.

"I know you and I are done. It doesn't stop me from thinking about you, but I'm not trying to get us back. I'm only here to make sure we are good." Janelle sat on the end of the couch, staring at the ground, chipping away at her cuticles.

"Janelle, you and I are sorors. Nothing else. I wish you happiness. Be careful who you decide to associate yourself with." Lauren leaned against the hotel door.

"With all due respect, I don't think who I associate myself with is any of your concern anymore. I don't want any problems." Janelle was paralyzed; she'd put everything she had into standing up for herself.

"Whatever you say," Lauren laughed.

"Don't laugh at me. These last two months have been hell. You want to be my friend, on my phone, but make sure I brutally understand we are not together. I fell in love with you." Janelle started pacing the room, and tears were building.

"So why are you here again?" Lauren grew annoyed.

"I don't know anymore. I thought..." Janelle paused. She looked at Lauren, radiating with irritation. "It doesn't matter what I thought. I need to say this. I went through depression and thought about killing myself more times than I want to admit. I can't go through anything more. I need us to be okay so I can move on."

"One sec," Lauren walked into the bathroom and returned with a small white cardboard box. She slammed it in Janelle's hand. "If you're going to do it, then do it, but don't blame it on me."

Janelle stared at the box of razors. Her tears stopped. Any love she had for Lauren was gone at that moment. *Who the fuck is this woman?* Janelle dropped the razors on the floor and walked towards the door. "No worries. I won't bother you again."

"Thank you, see you at the club," she closed the door behind Janelle. She searched her hotel room for her purse and phone. *Now I'm running behind. I should know better by now.*

TIFFANY TAPPED LAUREN on the shoulder while she waited at the bar for a bartender to give her their attention. Lauren turned around and wrapped her arms around her waist, pulling her in tight. She pushed back quickly.

"What do you want to drink? It's on me," Lauren offered.

"I'm not drinking tonight. I'm the sober soror," Tiffany refused.

"Pity, we could have had fun," Lauren responded. She traced one finger across Tiffany's hip and just below her stomach. She swatted Lauren's hand. The bartender asked them what they wanted. "I'll have a shot of tequila and whatever she wants."

"I don't want anything, thank you," she waved off the bartender. "I'm going to find my sorors. You have fun."

"I plan to," Lauren turned to her shot and swallowed it before passing her card to the bartender.

The club was dark but softly lit with dim LED lights in the rainbow across the ceiling. The bar spanned the entire wall, with tables separating it from the dance floor. VIP took up the opposite wall, sectioned off with velvet ropes and security. The sorors and bruhs were the special guests for the night, and the VIP was all theirs. Each VIP table had bottles of vodka, tequila, and whiskey settled in ice. Most of them were on the dance floor or standing on the side watching. Janelle was nestled in the corner of VIP.

"Hey, why are you over here by yourself," Nicole asked.

"I feel better over here," she responded.

"Come dance with me," Nicole grabbed her hand and pulled her up. "Please!"

Nicole started swinging her hips to the music. Her hips peaked through the splits of her black knee-length dress, greeted Janelle's eyes, and her curves swayed back and forth. Nicole led her to the dance floor, where her slow grinding stunned Janelle. She pulled her hands, slipping them under her dress to where her thighs met. They danced together for a few moments. Nicole tightened their connection when she turned around and wrapped her arms around Janelle's neck, her face drawn to the curve of Nicole's neck, inhaling her.

"I had fun with you last night," Nicole's whispers tickled Janelle's ear; she felt her soft, wet tongue exploring her neck.

"I had a good time too, damn," Janelle's hands roamed Nicole's body, creating a drumbeat between her legs.

"You should come back to our room tonight," Nicole asked.

"I can't; I'm hanging with Brittani," Janelle said.

"I know," she tucked her hand under Janelle's top until she found her nipple. Janelle froze, afraid someone would see them, but more afraid she would stop. The music wrapped around them, creating a pocket in time. Janelle danced as the heat between her legs grew. Nicole's fingers teased her erect nipples and sent surges through her body. It was like nothing she'd ever experienced before. She nestled her face in Nicole's neck and rocked back and forth with her. Her breaths were shorter, deeper. "She'll be there too."

Janelle pulled back, looking at Nicole with confusion, "Brittani's going to be in your room tonight?"

"I was hoping both of you would," Nicole pulled her back in and whispered in her ear, her fingers still playing with her nipples. She pressed on them, creating pleasure from pressure and then pain. A small explosion erupted between Janelle's thighs, weakening her knees. She struggled to catch her breath as Nicole kissed her.

"I'll have to talk to Brittani," Janelle whispered. She stumbled off the dance floor towards her table. She cupped her face in her hands when she landed in her chair. *What the fuck is going on? Why does she feel so good?*

"Are you trying to embarrass me," Lauren stood behind Janelle, staring straight into the crowd so no one would notice her words. "Because I don't like to be embarrassed."

"What?" Janelle jumped in her seat but was still too intoxicated to stand up. She held her head down, hoping Lauren would walk away. She didn't.

"What's going on with you and Nicole?" Lauren asked as she claimed the seat across from Janelle, smiling like their conversation was enjoyable.

"Nothing, we were just dancing," Janelle had a small, almost unnoticeable shiver. She whispered, "Why does it matter?"

"It matters because Nicole has something sneaky going on, and I don't trust her. Neither should you," Lauren whispered, rubbing Janelle's thigh, attempting to calm her. "I don't want anyone to use you to get to me."

"No one knows about us or what we were. That's how you wanted it." Janelle crossed her legs, shifting Lauren's hand off her.

"Just don't bother with her. She's not worth it and leave Brittani alone, too. They have some weird group thing going on. It's for your own good." She stood in front of Janelle and caressed her face. Janelle flinched. "I wouldn't do anything to hurt you."

"Too late," Janelle pushed past her and walked towards the women's restroom. Her rushed, tense sprint across the dance floor caught Brittani's attention. *Something is wrong.* Brittani hurried to console Janelle, but she snatched away and begged to be left alone. She followed anyway.

Lauren checked her phone for the time; her attention was drawn to the girl from the pledge line with the white socks dancing alone on the dance floor. Her tongue gently traced her own lips while she held Lauren's eye contact. Her hands went up her thighs, traced her shorts, up her hips, across her stomach, her crop top rising, her hands on her own breasts. *Yep, I know what this means.*

"You're not even two days old yet, and you're already acting up," Lauren pushed the young woman into the men's restroom. She hadn't seen a man in the club, so she figured it would be safe.

Her pale skin shimmered in the dim restroom light. She giggled at Lauren's scolding and lifted her crop top over her head. She licked her lips, licked two fingers, and then they disappeared under her shorts. Her thighs spread slightly; she let out a soft moan while she massaged her breast and rocked back and forth. Her legs almost released her, but she leaned back on the restroom wall for support. She never stopped looking at Lauren, and Lauren didn't move. She pulled her hand out of her shorts, her fingers glistening with her arousal. Then, she unzipped her shorts, and they slid down her legs to the floor. Standing only in a pink sheer bra and pink stilettos, she silently dared Lauren to take her. Lauren didn't flinch. The young woman's fingers disappeared inside her over and over, slowly, with long, deep strokes. She had difficulty muffling her own moans, and the last one was too strong for her.

"Oh fuck!" she yelled, forcing Lauren to cover her mouth with her hand. She could feel her chest rising and falling, riding her orgasm like a wave crashing into Lauren. "I'm Shana."

Lauren wrapped her fingers around Shana's neck, and her eyes rolled into the back of her head. Her fingers, still inside her, continued to stroke faster and faster. Her struggling breaths sent shockwaves through Lauren's thighs. This time, Shana didn't make a sound; her entire body bucked, and she leaked down her own hand. Lauren released her, allowing her to stand on her own. Shana collected her clothes and ducked into a stall. She quickly cleaned herself up, and without a word, Lauren left the restroom.

Janelle hid behind the women's restroom door, waiting for Lauren to pass, holding Brittani behind her. She couldn't take another interaction with her. *That's weird.* Lauren stopped, then shook her head and whispered, "Fucking neos."

When Lauren was no longer in view, Janelle and Brittani slowly exited the restroom. *Get yourself together, girl. This is not the look. Don't let that woman throw you off like this. You can handle this.*

"Are you good?" Brittani caressed her cheek. The struggle with Lauren had worn her down for months, and she wanted to release Janelle from the hold.

"I'm good; give me a minute, and I'll meet you in VIP." Brittani smiled and tapped Janelle on her butt. She kissed her on the forehead and walked away.

Before Janelle could start down the hallway, a light-skinned woman exited the men's restroom, tugging at her crop top that was stuck under her bra in the back. Janelle quickly pulled her shirt free, and she turned around to introduce herself.

"Oh my gosh, thank you. I'm Shana. You're Janelle, right?" Her full pink lips curled into a smile.

"Yeah, I'm Janelle. Nice to meet you, Shana. How's your first full day as a Nu Nu Lambda?" she repeated the same question she asked all the neos.

"Exhilarating," Shana smirked. "This sorority is going to be so much fun."

Her excitement dripped from every part of her, but it wasn't for the sisterhood or the service to the community. Her eyes resembled a wolf staring into a field of sheep as she gleamed about her future in the organization. The two women walked back into the club with small talk. Shana asked Janelle about every sister she could find in the crowd.

"That's Kelsey. She's cool, but she can be a bit much sometimes, but that's just for me. That's Lynette, Kaitlyn, and Di dancing near VIP together. If you want to know everything about Nu Nu Lambda, those three are the ones to talk to. They are our historian, social media manager, and PR person." She kept going, listing generic points for each soror. She even pointed to a few bruhs but warned Shana to stay away from them for anything other than business for the first year. "And you know Lauren, right?"

"We've met," she smiled. Janelle smirked, told Shana she was headed back to VIP, and she was free to join her. They took two shots together and continued chatting. Brittani lingered in the background with the two of them, pouring drinks and making sure they were safe. Shana was starting to reek of alcohol, and her speech was clearly slurred. She tried to stand up to dance after yelling that this was her song but quickly sat back down when she realized how drunk she was. "She's leaving. I was hoping to have her face between my legs tonight."

Janelle searched the doors and found Lauren sneaking out the side door. *At least she's consistent.* Janelle pulled two bottles of water out of the ice. She turned the first bottle over into Shana's mouth, letting it spill down her chin, neck, and chest. The cool feeling would sober her up a bit. When the entire bottle was gone, Janelle cracked the second bottle open and put it into Shana's hand, and gave her 'the you better drink this' look. Shana reluctantly nodded her head.

"You probably should stay away from Lauren too. She's the president, you know?" Janelle warned her.

"She already made me cum harder than I ever have, and she didn't touch me." Shana confidently slurred. Her head was bouncing from side to side, and her eyelids were fighting to stay open.

"Try resting on this couch." Shana agreed.

The couch must have been comfortable because as soon as she sat down, she fell asleep. Janelle alerted another soror sitting in VIP rubbing ice cubes on her chest to keep an eye out for the neo. The club was starting to slow down a bit, especially with most of the sorors and bruhs hugging up in corners or already headed back to their hotel rooms. Saturday night was notoriously the hookup night of every event. If anyone was going to get into trouble, it usually happened Saturday night.

She searched the dance floor for Brittani, afraid her time was running out. She spotted her on the other end of the bar whispering with Melinda. *Damn, where did all my sorors go? One, two, three, only three left here.* She started towards Brittani and noticed there were still quite a few bruhs spread out in the club, pushing up on the Miami women or each other. *Is that Aaron and Ambber?*

"Hey Janelle," Melinda smiled. She lightly caressed Janelle's arm while her other hand was tucked into Brittani's jeans. Brittani didn't move; she just stared at Janelle, waiting for her response.

"Hi, what's going on here?" Janelle grinned at the two of them.

"The beginning of something beautiful. Right, Brit?" She couldn't answer because Melinda kissed her passionately, then turned to Janelle and kissed her softly, waiting for her invitation for more. Janelle leaned into the kiss; she felt Brittani's lips on her neck.

"So, I guess you are coming to our room tonight," Nicole laughed. They turned to her mischievous grin. "This is going to be fun."

Chapter 7

A black SUV pulled up to the side door of the club; Lauren matched the license plate from a text and jumped in. She'd received a text message a few hours earlier with instructions for the evening, including the time her ride would meet her outside the club.

She used the time to touch up her makeup and calm her nerves. Her heart was beating in her ears, and she couldn't seem to regulate her breathing. Her phone dinged with another text message. *'The door is open; come in, take off all your clothes, and put on the blindfold.'* The SUV slowly approached a single-family home that was completely dark. Small solar-powered lights traced the walkway to two bronze pillars, introducing the front door. It was indeed unlocked, and Lauren walked right in. The foyer was dark, but a small light flickered at the end of the hallway. Lauren followed only one line of instructions.

The room was dimly lit with layers of rose petals leading to the jacuzzi and bed. The air was still thick with steam and expensive cologne. A red satin blindfold was sitting on the bed. Lauren looked around and found no one. The room and bathroom were empty. She undressed, hung her clothes in the closet, and reluctantly covered her eyes with the soft satin after sitting on the edge of the bed. She was left waiting only 30 seconds before footsteps knocking on the hardwood floors approached her. The scent of the expensive cologne grew stronger until Bae was standing right in front of her. Soft lips kissed hers. Strong fingers gripped her locs. She let out a soft sigh. The firm tug on her hair directed her to stand. She complied. She was turned around; cold, hard metal snapped around her wrists, restraining her. She was pushed onto a triangle on the bed that propped her ass in the air and her head on the bed.

"Now, we may begin," a strong raspy voice announced.

THE MORNING SUN STABBED into their bedroom, interrupting their rest. Lauren cuddled into her lover's body, hoping to extend her time here. A strong, muscular arm wrapped around her and pulled her in closer until she was lying on top of her lover.

"Good morning," Dani said in her ear.

"Good morning, Bae," Lauren pouted. "I thought you were still asleep."

"Not with that sun beating me up, but it seems like he was waiting for you to wake up," Dani cupped Lauren's ass and pressed into her. Lauren let out a soft moan. She could feel Dani growing under her. They kissed passionately, their naked skin merging them. Lauren slid him inside her slowly; she was startled by the size. She rode him with one hand on his chest and the other pinching her own nipple. His hands gripped her ass, fingertips dug into her skin. *Fuck!* He raised his hips to control their movement faster and harder. Their bodies buckled as they both came with him inside her.

"Oh fuck. I didn't know you could do that." Lauren lay beside Dani and stroked him. "You are a grower, for sure."

"Aren't most transguys growers?" Dani laughed. "Seeing you has been so much more than I could have ever imagined."

"I wish I could have been right here with you the whole weekend. When am I going to see you again?" Lauren kissed Dani's sweaty abs.

"Soon. I have to see what my schedule looks like," Dani responded.

"My busy businessman," Lauren kissed up Dani's stomach, to his chest, neck, and then his lips. She lingered in their kiss until he pulled back. He leaned away to check the time on his phone, 10:22 am.

"It's time for us to get up," Dani pulled himself from Lauren and started rustling through his suitcase. He pulled out a pair of underwear and disappeared into the bathroom without another word. Lauren sat on the bed and pulled the sheet to cover her exposed body. Twenty minutes went by. She didn't move. He emerged from the bathroom wearing his boxer briefs, still damp from his shower. "Are you okay?"

"Yeah, Bae. I was just waiting for you," Lauren lied. She threw the sheet off and stood up on the bed. "One more taste before I go back into president mode?"

"Tempting, but I have a lunch to get to before I head to the airport. Don't you have something with your org?" Dani patted his body with a towel and covered himself with a white t-shirt and black slim-fit jeans.

"You're right. I only have about 45 minutes before the ladies start showing up at the restaurant." Lauren jumped off the bed, grabbed her clothes from last night, and closed herself in the bathroom. She finished 20 minutes later. She jumped on Dani, "I guess this is see you later."

"It will be no time before we see each other again." Dani held Lauren in his arms and kissed her before setting her down. Lauren rushed around the room, collecting all her things. She picked up a bottle of Dior perfume, thinking it was hers, but it wasn't. *It is a woman's perfume, hmm. I wonder who this belongs to.*

"Ok, bae, let me get out of here. My Uber is outside. See you later," Lauren kissed Dani, glanced at the perfume, and left.

"WAKEY, WAKEY, SLEEPY head," Nicole planted soft pecks all over Janelle's face until she woke up. "There you are."

"Mmmm, hey," Janelle rubbed her eyes to wake all the way up; she was unsuccessful. She turned over and saw Brittani still hugged up with Melinda on the other side of the bed. She shook her head, smiled, and tried to doze off.

"Really, it's time to get up. We don't have much time," Nicole shook her. She cut her eyes at Nicole and sat up.

"They are still asleep," she whined, pointing to Melinda and Brittani.

"And they will take half the time of one of us. You still have to go back to your room and get your stuff together," Nicole scolded. Janelle searched the room and pointed to her suitcase, which was neatly settled in the corner of the hotel room.

"Melinda took care of it for me last night," she smiled; Nicole jumped on top of her, tickling her. Janelle tried to resist but instead started kissing her to distract her. They lay back on the bed, kissing and rubbing each other. Janelle pulled back with hesitation in her eyes. "Lauren wasn't happy to see me with you last night."

"I'm sure. She is terrified of me because I'm married to Melinda. I'm probably the only soror that doesn't have a position that makes her stop in her tracks for something other than sex." Nicole laughed. "You are fine; if she does anything to you, she knows I will come for her."

"I went to see her yesterday to talk to her to make sure we were ok," Janelle trailed off and looked at her fidgeting fingers.

"What did she do?" Nicole lifted her eyes. "Tell me."

"Nothing. I tried to talk to her and tell her what had happened with me mentally over the last couple of months, and when I told her, I thought about killing myself..." Janelle paused.

"What, Janelle?" Nicole sat up and gripped Janelle's wrist.

"She gave me a box of razors and told me to do it if I want to, but don't blame her," Janelle whispered, tears running down her cheeks.

"Fuck her! You hear me," Nicole grabbed her face. "You are a beautiful, smart, talented woman. So, fuck everything about her!"

Melinda was startled by the cursing; she peaked at the two of them with one eye open. Nicole waved her back to sleep; everything was ok. She turned over and held Brittani until she fell back asleep.

"She told me to stay away from you and Melinda. Said that you two were into weird group things, and it wasn't good for me," Janelle continued.

"We are poly, that's it," Nicole scoffed. "She has the nerve with all the broken hearts she leaves in her path."

"I don't want any trouble. She can cause so much for me if I make her upset." Janelle lay back on the bed.

"I'll take care of her," Nicole kissed Janelle on the forehead and went into the bathroom. Janelle heard the shower running. She cuddled in bed with Brittani and Melinda and fell back asleep.

Chapter 8

"Ladies! Ladies! Can I have your attention, please," Lauren stood at the head of three tables covered with empty plates filled with sorors and bruhs, reminiscing over the weekend, laughing, and taking photos. The rest of The Broken Egg was quiet compared to the sorors and bruhs. They all paused and gave her their attention. "This is the end of the 2024 Biennial National Convention. We were successful in crossing 12 sorors and six bruhs. Welcome to the fam, neos."

They all stood in applause for the neos. The new additions to the family all blushed and thanked their organization. High fives, hugs, laughter, and sad faces spread through the crowd. Janelle was cuddled between Nicole and Brittani at the far end of a table. Melinda sat on the other side of Nicole. The four of them looked like they were in their own world, only looking up when Lauren talked and when Shana jumped in from across the table.

"We didn't have any positions that required voting, so it made things a little more relaxed this year. The two boards concluded a total of 6 meetings this weekend without interrupting any of the family fun activities. Two were completed without my attendance for the first time in our family history. Give yourself a hand," Lauren clapped towards the board members, showing individual appreciation. The board members stuck out like sore thumbs during their recognition; they clapped harder than anyone else, stood when no one else did, and continued longer than necessary. "Okay, okay. I hope everyone here made lasting bonds and memories and plans for your future in this family. I enjoyed meeting all the new faces and loved seeing all my prophytes. This right here, being all together, this is my why. This right here is what keeps me going, keeps me striving for the best for this family. I love y'all!"

The restaurant was filled with roaring applause, stomping, and cheering. Everyone returned to their individual conversations. Exchanging phone numbers, social media handles, and any other forms of communication they could find. Lauren sat down and enjoyed the moment. She noticed Kelsey sitting by herself at the end of one of their tables. She wasn't talking to anyone; her plate was still full of food. *It can't be me checking on her; she'll think it means I want her back.* Lauren searched for Tiffany; she'd be the perfect neutral party to handle Kelsey. When she did find Tiffany, she was heading toward the exit. She had a large smile on her face, and she was moving quickly, looking at something outside. Lauren followed her line of sight and saw a muscular chocolate man waiting with open arms. *Dani?* Tiffany jumped into his arms, and their kiss lingered; Lauren felt a rock in her chest move toward her throat. *Nope, not here.*

Lauren waved the server over to her and handed the heavy-set brunette woman the sorority credit card to cover the bill for all three tables. She waited for her to return with her receipt. Gave her a hefty tip. *We are a lot to deal with for any restaurant.* She gathered her purse, said her goodbyes to a few sorors and bruhs, and made one last stop at the restroom. She nervously adjusted her clothes and checked her makeup in the bathroom mirror before heading out.

"So, you weren't going to say goodbye?" Dani stopped her as she exited the women's restroom.

"I said my goodbyes when I left you this morning. You seem to have your hands full now. I don't want to make anything more complicated for myself." Lauren swung her locs off her shoulder and continued, "I hope you enjoy the rest of your day."

"It doesn't bother you, does it?" Dani scoffed.

Lauren paused and considered turning around and cursing Dani out for having her in this situation. Instead, she stood straight up, shook off whatever Dani was trying to put on her, and continued walking. Her chest was caving in on her, and she was holding her breath to stay standing, let alone walking. She walked through every phone conversation, Facetime, and virtual date they'd had. *Not one time was there any evidence of a girlfriend or a wife.* Her new sorors ran up to her to hug and say goodbye. The rest of her time in the restaurant was a blur. She did everything she was expected to do and said everything she was supposed to say. And she left without a word to Tiffany. She just left.

LAUREN SUNK INTO HER window seat on the large aircraft. She turned towards the window and pulled a blanket up to her neck. She was one of the first ones on the flight due to her early pre-check. People flooded the aisle, rushing to catch a seat in the front or find a place to stash their oversized carry-on.

Random conversations about Miami Beach, restaurants, and secret rendezvous buzzed up and down the aisle. *Is anyone I know on my flight?* It wasn't long before she received her answer.

"Hey babe," Sammie plopped in the seat next to her. "Why do you look like you're hiding from the feds?"

Lauren didn't move. She started breathing deeper to make the blanket movement obvious.

"Girl quit fucking playing with me. I know you're not sleeping." Sammie slapped Lauren's thigh.

"Oh fuck!" Lauren pushed Sammie and caressed her tender thigh. "What is wrong with you? You can't read the room. Did it seem like I wanted to talk?"

"I don't care. I'm on this flight with you and want to talk about the tea that came up at brunch. Why didn't you tell me you were fucking with Tiffany's wife? That shit had the entire Broken Egg lit up after you left," Sammie started in.

Sammie described Tiffany's face when one of the sorors followed them back from the restroom and told her their entire conversation. Tiffany snapped off on Dani, and it didn't seem like he cared. She went on for a moment, trying to figure out why Tiffany called him her wife if he was a guy. She settled on Tiffany trying to throw the organization off since she never brought him around before. She wondered why he showed up this time after all these years. Lauren was looking at the plane's wing and wishing Sammie would shut up. She thought about Kelsey, Janelle, and Sammie. Shana popped into her mind. *How could I have let this weekend get away from me like that? That shit is not like me at all. Fuck Dani.* Sammie continued talking about Janelle and Brittani, how fucked up Brittani was for treating her so badly at the beach, and she didn't come to see her that night either. She told Lauren her suspicions about Melinda, Nicole, Brittani, and Janelle having a poly relationship because someone told her they saw them together last night. She started laughing and blurted out Brittani is fucking with Ambber, her bruh. She turned to Lauren to reassure herself that everything she had said was not to be repeated, but Lauren fell asleep for real this time. Her head was smashed against the plane window. Sammie tucked her pillow under Lauren's head and pulled out her laptop. *Time for some Netflix.*

LAUREN SWUNG OPEN HER front door, dropped her bags on the living room floor, and pulled out her cell phone. *No missed calls, no messages, nothing.* She pulled up Dani's contact that read *Bae.* She opened their text thread and scrolled through all the loving, supportive, sweet messages she had been receiving for months. She started typing and realized this was too much to put in text on someone else's phone. She called Dani. *No answer.* She left him a voicemail telling him to call her back as soon as he got this; they had something to figure out. She stood in the middle of her living room, staring at her home and feeling like her body was filling with flammable liquid. *Just one spark.*

She checked her notifications again. *No calls, no messages.* She tapped Dani's name and called him again. *No answer. Tiffany will be all over Dani after finding out about me. She is not going to let him answer. I have to find another way to contact him.* Lauren pulled her laptop out of her carry-on and opened her email. She searched for Dani's work email address and typed out everything she needed to say while still respecting his job. *I won't get a response tonight.* She pulled off the rest of her clothes and jumped into the shower.

Chapter 9

*D*ing. *Ding. Ding.* Lauren's phone was vibrating across her nightstand. It was 9 am, and she'd slept well.

Six text messages, two emails, and nine phone calls. What the fuck is going on? She opened the emails. *One from Dani and one from the board of Nu Nu Lambda Sorority, Inc.* She opened the email from Dani first. He explained that Tiffany and his marriage was open, and he didn't realize she was the president of Tiffany's organization. *Liar.* He still wanted to spend time with her but wasn't sure how she felt about it. He expressed Tiffany's disdain for their relationship, but she would never try to control whom he interacted with. Dani ended the email with I love you, Dani. *Love?*

She opened the email from her sorority next. *Dear Ms. Jacobson, We regret to inform you...* Lauren's body felt like it was on fire. They alerted her to accusations of inappropriate interactions with pledges and neophytes. They quoted their bylaws that stated anyone on the board was prohibited from having romantic or sexual contact with pledges or neophytes due to the uneven power dynamics. It also referenced expectations of favoritism and a meeting on Tuesday at 7 pm. *There was no way they were going to go this far without proof. Who was it?* Lauren calmed herself, made a cup of coffee, and sat at her computer. She silenced her phone. *I'm not ready to make a statement. Everything I say is a statement.* She opened her university website and started on a paper that was due soon.

"SHE IS GOING TO THINK this was me!" Janelle yelled at her phone. Brittani facetimed her this morning when she started getting phone calls about Lauren's email. She explained it all to Janelle and tried to reassure her it wouldn't fall back on her. Janelle was convinced, "How is this not going to blow back on me? I didn't tell y'all anything to push a sanction."

"I know you didn't. This has nothing to do with you, Janelle. You didn't officially report anything. One of your sorors is providing evidence. You haven't heard about Kelsey, have you?" Janelle's demeanor softened; her brows wrinkled in concern.

"What happened to Kelsey?" she asked.

"Kelsey was put on a 72-hour psych hold. She took a bunch of pills last night when she got home. Her mom found her almost dead. She swears she didn't try to kill herself, but it looks like she did." Tears welled up in Brittani's eyes.

"Because of Lauren. I know it was because of Lauren," Janelle shook her head.

"I don't know. She's been going through a lot of bruhs over the last few weeks. I mean traveling all over the country to visit anyone that would give her their attention. I guess the event was too much for her. They said she told them she was trying to go to sleep because she hadn't slept for real in weeks. Can sleep deprivation do that to you?" Brittani asked.

Janelle didn't answer. She just stared blankly into the phone. *That could have been me. I was so depressed. It didn't feel worth it. She wouldn't leave me alone.* "Hey, did anyone get Kelsey's phone?"

"I think her parents have all her stuff," Brittani responded.

"How did Kelsey have something to do with Lauren's email?" Janelle inquired.

"Kelsey's mom saw a message between Kelsey and Lauren. They upset her, so she forwarded them to Tiffany. Apparently, Tiffany has been visiting Kelsey and being there for her during this time. Who knew." Brittani threw her hands in the air.

"So, Tiffany sent the texts to the rest of the board?" The picture was finally coming together. "Is she the soror that reported Lauren?"

"No, but you won't believe this. You know that new soror Shana?" Brittani asked.

"Yeah," she chuckled.

"She went to her big sister, Jessica, and told her that Lauren pulled her into the men's restroom, choked her, and made her masturbate in front of her. Isn't that crazy?" Brittani kept talking. She went on about how Lauren didn't look like the type, but she knew you couldn't tell by just looking at people. She said Shana was uncomfortable with Lauren being the president with so many impressionable women under her, hoping to please her. They said she begged the board to do something about this because Lauren seemed too comfortable with what she did for this to be the first time. "After what happened with Kelsey, Shana's accusations were just icing on the cake."

"So, they are removing Lauren as president?" Janelle's knees gave out on her; she fell back on her couch and put all her energy into holding her phone.

"I'm not sure if that will be it. She might not be able to hold a position, let alone stay in the org." Brittani was starting to look like she was enjoying this.

"I have to call you back," Janelle hung up on her and immediately opened Nicole's contact. She tapped the facetime button and waited for her to answer. "What did you do?"

"Hi to you too with your beautiful self," Nicole answered. Melinda said hi from behind Nicole and walked off after kissing her on the cheek.

"Hey, Melinda. What did you do, Nicole?" she repeated.

"I didn't do anything. What are you talking about?" she held back a small grin.

Janelle sighed, "Nicole!"

"I didn't do anything. I just helped shed light on what someone else was doing to the women in our sorority. We are supposed to build each other up, not jump around beating each other down. Then, acting like the archetype of greatness. I told you I would take care of it," she carried a strength in her tone that Janelle had never heard before. She liked it. "Are you upset at me?"

"No...I'm not upset. I don't need this blowing back on me," Janelle admitted.

"It won't. Why don't you come to see us this weekend?" she offered.

"I just made it back home yesterday. I can't travel again," Janelle laughed.

"Why not? Do you have kids or pets, or are you responsible for your dying grandmother I don't know about?" she teased.

"Shut up," Janelle giggled. "You know what I mean. I can't buy a ticket that quick."

"I didn't ask you to purchase a ticket. Hold on." Nicole put the phone down. Her voice was far and muffled, but Janelle could make out parts of her conversation with Melinda. She seemed to agree with Janelle's visit. She asked if she should call Brittani. Nicole told her to call her; she didn't think Janelle was ready to interact with them on her own yet. When she picked up the phone, she continued, "OK, so how does Friday at 7:30 pm sound? That gives you plenty of time to make it to the airport after work. And the nonstop flight from Columbus to Atlanta is less than 2 hours. You can be comfortable here with us by 10 pm on Friday night."

Janelle just looked at the phone. She was sure the call froze until Janelle finally smiled. "Why do y'all want to buy me a flight?"

"I want to see you, and if I want to see you, then I'm going to fly you out. It's just that simple." She said with ease. "So, are you coming to see me or not?"

"Yeah, that sounds good," Janelle blushed.

"A car will pick you up at your house at 5 pm. I know it's about a 30-minute drive to the airport. You will have the full two hours to check in and get something to eat if you want before your flight." she ran down the itinerary she put together on the spot. Janelle's phone was vibrating one right after the other. Each one was an email with additional details about her trip.

"Wait, you still didn't tell me what you did," Janelle realized she was distracting her.

"I'll go through all of it when you get here, okay?" Nicole waited for her response.

"Fine. I'll see you on Friday," Janelle giggled.

"Good, now I have a meeting to get to. I probably won't talk to you much this week because we have a busy week in front of us, but it's all about you and me on Friday. I'll talk to you soon." Nicole blew a kiss into the phone and hung up.

Janelle felt sadness building in her chest. She scrolled through her contacts. *Lauren – President. She must be losing her mind right now. I saw Shana after Lauren left her, and she didn't seem like anyone had been assaulted. Shit, what the fuck am I saying. How does someone act like they were assaulted?* Janelle tossed her phone on the couch and walked into her bedroom. She pulled open her suitcase and separated her dirty clothes for laundry. As a third-grade teacher, she didn't have to return to work until August. The only thing she had planned today was her therapy appointment this afternoon. After this weekend, she couldn't skip it.

MONDAY WAS A BLUR FOR Lauren. She tried to work on her papers for school, but she couldn't focus. Being a full-time student with so many around to support her allowed her to stay away from traditional jobs for now, but it gave too much time for her mind to wander. She struggled to go to sleep Monday night, so when she woke up after 1 pm on Tuesday, she didn't think anything of it. She still hadn't heard Dani's voice or seen his face. She also didn't respond to his email. She knew he wouldn't put himself out there unless he were sure she was ready to move forward. *Fuck it, make this my time.* She pulled the cover over her head and tried to go back to sleep, but someone started banging on her front door. It was only a matter of time before someone showed up. No one had heard from her since she left the restaurant on Sunday. She didn't bother to cover her naked body or tie down her locs standing all over the place. She swung open the front door.

"What!" she yelled at Sammie. She turned around and went back into her bedroom. The cover was calling her.

"Bitch if you don't get your ass out of that bed. You have a meeting in less than six hours, and I know you haven't figured out what evidence they have." Sammie didn't bother to look at Lauren.

"I know who it is, and there's no way for me to prove I didn't do it. They don't put cameras in the men's restroom." Lauren peaked out the cover.

"Oh damn, you really did that shit?" Sammie whispered.

"I didn't assault Shana. I pulled her into the men's restroom to talk to her because she was getting all naked and shit on the dance floor. When we got in there, she started playing with herself. I just didn't stop her. I also didn't leave. She got too loud, and I didn't want anyone to catch me in there with her like that, so I covered her mouth. And yeah, I choked her when she came again, but she was into that shit," Lauren explained.

"Damn, babe." Sammie sat on Lauren's bed. "Well, I thought it was Kelsey."

"Kelsey would never go to the board about me," Lauren responded.

"I know. She tried to kill herself Sunday night," Sammie continued.

"What?" Lauren searched for her phone, but Sammie snatched it from the bed before she could get to it.

"You can't call her. Her mom sent everything to Tiffany. The org has your text messages with Kelsey. Everything. They're going to try to put that on you," Sammie reluctantly reported.

Lauren's face drained of all its color. She couldn't fathom Kelsey trying to do something like that, let alone be blamed for it. She knew Kelsey was having a hard time with the end of their interactions but *damn*. Now, with Kelsey and possibly Shana, Lauren knew she was buried. The only thing she could do at this point was damage control.

"Hello, are you there?" Sammie was waving her hand in front of Lauren's face. "Damn, can you see I'm right here?"

"Sorry, I was trying to figure out how I could limit the damage these women are going to cause me." Lauren jumped up, went through her drawers, and pulled out a pair of panties and a matching bra. She opened her closet and pulled out a blouse and joggers. Her meeting would be on video, so there is no need to dress up her bottom half. "Are you staying?"

"Hell yeah, I'm going to be here for your meeting and afterward. I'm going nowhere." Sammie crossed her arms and planted herself on Lauren's bed.

Lauren gave her the finger and rushed into the bathroom. Sammie could hear the shower running. She relocated to Lauren's living room with a glass of her white wine in front of her television. Lauren finished and glanced at Sammie as she made her way back to her bedroom, still damp. She locked herself in her bedroom after she grabbed her hard copy of the sorority's constitution and bylaws. Sammie helped herself to snacks from

Lauren's kitchen as Lauren continued to dig through information to find her way out. After five hours, Lauren emerged from her bedroom, fully dressed but without an answer.

"So, nothing, huh?" Sammie asked.

"I think they may have me. I fucked up messing with that neo. It's very clear in our bylaws that the sorority can't control matters of the heart. Even if they have proof I was messing with Kelsey, they can't prove we weren't in a relationship. All they can hit me with is not reporting. Shana, on the other hand. That shit seemed too good. It probably was a setup." Lauren tossed the stack of papers on her coffee table.

"Those women don't have big enough balls to set you up. It sounds like the wrong place at the wrong time." Sammie closed her cell phone after finishing up a text message.

"I don't know, but I have less than an hour before this meeting," Lauren sighed.

"Well," Sammie held up a blunt. "What about a session?"

"You know I don't fuck with that like that." Lauren refused.

"It may be time for you to start," Sammie waved the blunt in Lauren's face. She snatched it from her and lit it. The two of them lay back on the couch and finished smoking. They sipped wine until it was time for her meeting. Lauren's alarm went off on her phone. *It's time.*

Chapter 10

"Once you grab your bag, there's a black SUV waiting for you outside," Melinda's voice echoes over the phone to Janelle. "Can you hear me?"

"Yes, I heard you. Black SUV ready to bring me to you," Janelle laughed. The week rushed by in a puff of smoke. It was already Friday night, and she was making her way to baggage claim at the Atlanta International Airport.

"Right to me," Melinda repeated. "We are having some people over, so don't be surprised when you come in."

"Ok, I'll see you soon." Janelle hung up the phone. She waited for her luggage to come around the conveyor belt, picked it up, and made her way to the SUV. "Hi, I'm..."

"Ms. Harris, nice to meet you. I hope you had a comfortable flight," the driver collected Janelle's luggage, opened her door, and put her luggage in the trunk. She enjoyed 40 minutes of Atlanta's views, long but necessary due to her nerves standing on edge.

"Here we are, Ms. Harris," the driver jumped out of the SUV, pulled out her luggage, and opened her door to a large white home with a blue front door tucked behind large pillars.

"Thank you," Janelle walked up the walkway, peeping down each side of the street at the homes that were just as impressive as this one. Before she reached the front door, it opened.

"Hey, beautiful," Nicole danced in the doorway. Melinda made her way around to Janelle's luggage. "Come in; we have some people for you to meet."

Janelle was led into a large foyer with hardwood floors disappearing in each direction of the house. Bright lights lit each room, and music filled the air. She followed Nicole, took off her shoes, and ended up in the family room with a lot of people. Some she knew, and many she didn't.

"Here we are, everyone," Nicole announced, and everyone turned their attention to Janelle. Nicole started the introductions, "First, the bruhs, you know Brittani and Aaron. There's Ambber, Vice President of Nu Delta Xi. That's Kiana, their Executive Director. The sorors, there's Jessica, Tiffany, and her husband, Dani."

"I thought this was about us this weekend?" Janelle was confused. She heard someone turn off the water in the distance and then footsteps on the hardwood floor, moving towards them. It was Shana.

"And welcome our new soror, Shana," Nicole finished. "This weekend is about us. It is about all of us."

"This has something to do with that meeting on Tuesday, doesn't it?" Janelle looked around at everyone giggling or whispering.

"I told you I'd tell you what happened," Nicole started. "This is about the meeting on Tuesday."

"IT SOUNDS LIKE THE pizza is here," Sammie reached toward Lauren with the blunt, jumped up, and stumbled to the door. She slapped cash into the delivery guy's hand, tossed the pizza on the coffee table, and went into the kitchen to grab drinks. When she thought of Lauren sitting at home waiting for the meeting, a rock welled up in her throat, and her hands started to sweat.

The sorority board investigated the accusations without asking her side. A written statement from Shana about the incident at the club was their star piece of evidence. Concerns were expressed about Kelsey's mental health and Lauren's effect on her, but without Kelsey there to report she tried to kill herself, they couldn't include Lauren in that accusation. It didn't matter. Shana's statement was enough. Nu Nu Lambda's board removed Lauren from the position of president, revoked her eligibility to hold a position on the board for five years, and put her on membership probation for two years. If she had any inappropriate interactions with sorors during her probation she would be expunged from the sorority. That's no intake, no voting rights, no real benefits of the organization at all, just events, fees, and community service. She didn't take it well. She lost her composure for the first time. Instead of taking the punishment, she gave up her letters that night. She wrote a letter resigning from the organization and spilled all of the board members' secrets.

"How do you feel?" Sammie asked her while they lay on the floor puffing indica and eating pizza.

"I feel...free. Like I can do whatever I want. Like I can do only what I want," Lauren laughed. "I am so fucking mad, and those bitches will pay for what they did, but I feel like they did me a favor too."

"Really? You didn't do what you wanted when you were in the sorority?" Sammie was a bit thrown off. It seemed like Lauren did everything she wanted.

"There's a lot I couldn't do because of the org. I know I created them; I am proud of them. People are hard to please. It doesn't matter how hard I work; someone is going to have something to complain about. I was sick of hearing sorors say how they could do things better, but no one ran for a position at the Convention either. No one wanted to take on responsibility without me walking them through it. I had to appoint everyone to their position.

"Damn. I didn't know it was like that," Sammie shook her head.

"Most people don't. If our event fees didn't cover the event, that money came out of my personal account when the org didn't have it. It was up to me to do everything when y'all didn't feel like it," Lauren's body sunk into the floor, the air around her pressed on her entire body like a weighted blanket.

"Would you do it again?" she asked with a large inhale.

"What, start an organization?" Lauren asked.

"Yeah, would you start another sorority?" she sat up and looked at Lauren.

Lauren paused; her red eyes darted around the room, and a small smile stretched across her face.

"YOU SET THIS ENTIRE thing up?" Janelle squinted at Nicole.

"No, I just helped things along," Nicole tapped Janelle on her arm and laughed.

"What?" Janelle was more confused than before.

"Tiffany and I are good friends. She told me about Kelsey and Lauren. About Kelsey sleeping around the frat because her feelings were hurt. I saw you and Lauren, but I needed Brittani to confirm it for me." Nicole hugged Melinda.

"Y'all tell the people you're sleeping with everything," Melinda continued. "All I had to do was wait for the bruhs to keep bringing me information until Nicole had what she needed."

"I didn't think Kelsey was that unstable," Nicole's boastful inflation dissipated, tears collected.

"I was with her almost every day. I didn't make it to see her the Sunday we got back because of the stuff with Lauren and Dani. That was on me," Tiffany hung her head and curled her shoulders in, but Dani drew her eyes up by her chin.

"It's not your fault. You did everything you could." Dani laid Tiffany's head on his chest. "She's doing fine. She's back home. She has a therapist, and they are working on getting her to her best self."

"To be honest, babe, Lauren did most of it for us. I knew she wouldn't be able to resist Shana, so I made sure she was on the pledge line, and Lauren did the rest," Nicole laughed, then pulled Melinda's arms around her, resting her back on Melinda's chest.

"You didn't think I had on white socks because I'm stupid when everything...everywhere said wear all black," Shana joined Nicole laughing. "For real, that went way better than I thought. I didn't expect her to start choking me. I mean, that shit felt good, but I didn't ask for all that."

"And y'all knew about all of this?" Janelle turned to the rest of the guests standing around them.

"I just did what I always do," Aaron rubbed her hands together and chuckled. "Our parties are legendary."

"I'm sure they are. That was something else," Janelle winked at Aaron. *Virile, that's the bruh that was checking Brittani out.* "Were we just part of the setup?"

Brittani rushed towards Janelle, wrapped their fingers together, and said, "You and me...that's the best part of all this. The only thing we were surprised about. I didn't expect to build anything with you. But I can't ignore how I feel. I'm falling in love with you."

Janelle sucked in a large gust of air and slowly exhaled, "I love you too, Brittani."

"Awe! I love that!" Shana jumped up and down and landed in Aaron's arms. Small matching rose gold bands on their fingers caught the light and Janelle's attention.

"Bitch, is this your wife?" Janelle snatched Shana's finger and held it in front of her face like it was the first time Shana had seen it. Shana burst into laughter.

"Girl, yes. Aaron is my wife. But we are all polyamorous. My daddy likes studs, so she is with Ambber. She messed with Kelsey, too, but before we knew about all this." Shana settled her small frame into Aaron's large arms. "I mean, you know about Brittani and Melinda, right?"

"Yeah, I just didn't..." Janelle paused and looked around at all the eyes on her. She was overwhelmed with the information. "...I'm going to need a moment to let all this settle in."

"That's completely understandable. Let me show you to your room." Nicole held Janelle's hand, leading her down the hallway. Brittani picked up her suitcase and followed.

"Are you okay?" Brittani sat next to Janelle on her queen-sized bed.

"Yeah, it's just a lot to take in," she responded. Nicole kissed her on the forehead and waved at them before slipping out of the bedroom. "You're happy here?"

"I've never felt more like myself," Brittani smiled at her. "It's not just sex and events. It's about real love for our sorors and bruhs. We're a family. We help each other with school, work, and businesses; it's about our success."

"Now, I'm one of y'all?" she looked up at Brittani.

"Now you're one of us," Brittani sealed her response with a kiss.

THE END

A Word from the Author

Thank you so much for reading Soror Love! This is just the beginning of a new series and collection to come. If you enjoyed this story, could you leave a review? Make sure to follow for updates and exclusives!
Instagram and Tiktok - @AuthorPhree

Don't miss out!

Visit the website below and you can sign up to receive emails whenever Shaun J. Phree publishes a new book. There's no charge and no obligation.

https://books2read.com/r/B-A-VVFM-EFPSC

BOOKS 2 READ

Connecting independent readers to independent writers.